Hic!
Hic!
Hic!
Hic!
Hic!
Hic!
Hic!
Hic!
Hic!
Hic!

Hannah's Hanukkah HICCUPS

By Shanna Silva
Illustrated by Bob McMahon

For Mom, Dad, Josh, Avi, and Daniel, with love.
— SS

To Lalane and Tyler, who help me through all of life's hiccups.
— BM

Hannah's Hanukkah Hiccups contains many different hiccup remedies; some of the cures are culturally specific, some have a medical basis, and some are folklore. All made for great fun in writing this book!
—SS

Apples & Honey Press
An imprint of Behrman House Publishers, 11 Edison Place, Springfield, New Jersey 07081
www.applesandhoneypress.com

ISBN 978-1-68115-537-1

Library of Congress Cataloging-in-Publication Data

Names: Silva, Shanna, author. | McMahon, Bob, 1956- illustrator.
Title: Hannah's Hanukkah hiccups / by Shanna Silva ; illustrated by Bob McMahon.
Description: Springfield, NJ ; Apples & Honey Press, an imprint of Behrman House, [2017] | Summary: "Hannah gets hiccups! Will they go away in time for her Hanukkah performance?"--Provided by publisher.
Identifiers: LCCN 2017012847 | ISBN 9781681155371
Subjects: | CYAC: Hiccups--Fiction. | Hanukkah--Fiction.
Classification: LCC PZ7.S585644 Han 2017 | DDC [E]--dc23 LC record available at https://lccn.loc.gov/2017012847

Edited by Ann Koffsky
Design by Terry Taylor Studio
Printed in China

9 8 7 6 5 4 3 2 1

It was almost Hanukkah. Some folks in the brownstone on Hester Street polished menorahs, fried potato latkes, or wrapped gifts. Others cleaned their apartments, played the piano, or napped.

In apartment 4H, Hannah Hope Hartman was rehearsing a song for her religious school's Hanukkah program.

She'd been practicing for weeks.

As she sang, she spun her dreidel across the floor, watching it settle under the table.

When she crouched to grab it, she erupted in hiccups.

She marched into the den, hiccuping with each step.

"I have—**HIC**—the hiccups," she giggled.

"Try holding your breath," her brother, Henry, suggested.

Hannah took a deep breath, puffing out her cheeks.

"**Boo!**" Henry shouted, startling her. But her hiccups continued.

The next day,
Hannah was
still hiccuping!
She tried to
ignore her
hiccups.

When Henry made silly faces, Hannah shrieked with laughter, making her hiccup even more.

Hannah's neighbors heard her hiccups through the building's thin walls. "Drink pickle juice backward," Mr. Taylor called up the stairwell from the creaky fourth step.

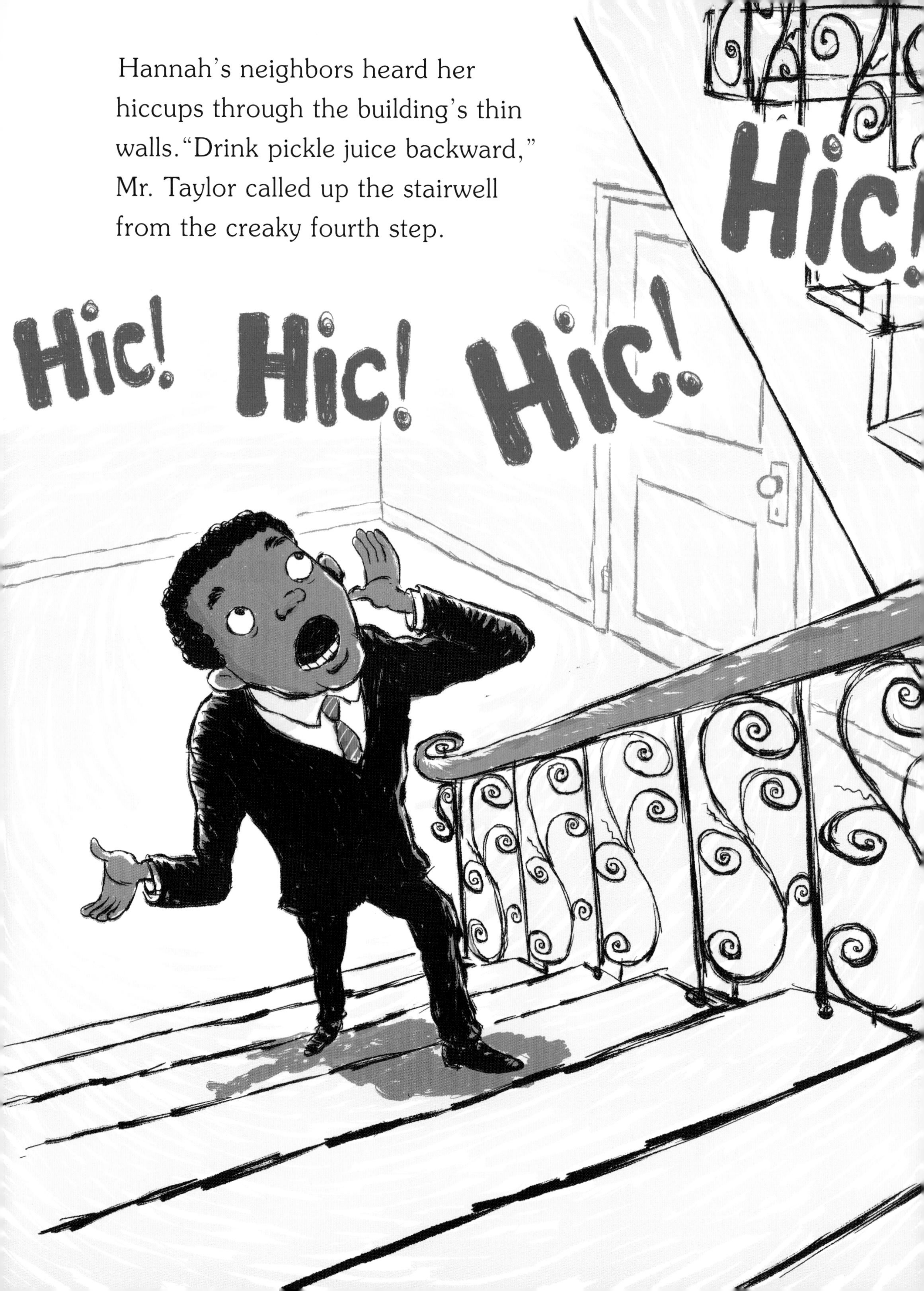

"Okay, Mr. Taylor," Hannah called, still laughing. She poured a glass of kosher dill juice and slurped from the far side of the glass.

"**HICCUP!**" Hannah frowned.

Later, Hannah's family lit their menorah for the first night of Hanukkah. Hannah hiccuped through the blessings. "I can't believe I'm still—**HIC**—hiccuping! It's not so funny any—**HIC**—more."

“What about my solo?” Hannah asked. Her puppy, Babka, whimpered at her side.

On the second night of Hanukkah, Mom said, “Don’t worry— your show is still seven days away; your hiccups will be gone.”

But on the third day of Hanukkah, Hannah was still hiccuping as she sat in the doctor's exam room.

"What's wrong, Hannah?" Dr. Silver asked.

"I can't—**HIC**—stop hiccuping!" Hannah answered.

Dr. Silver listened to Hannah's heartbeat.
He tapped her knee with a small hammer.
He shined a light into her ears.

"Hannah, you have the hiccups,"
Dr. Silver announced.

"I—**HIC**—know!"
Hannah exclaimed.

Dr. Silver pulled a paper bag from his lab coat pocket and passed it to Hannah.

"Breathe into the bag," he said. The bag crinkled as Hannah inhaled and exhaled.

For a moment she was quiet. But only for a moment.

"HICCUP!"

"What—**HIC**—should I do?" Hannah asked.

"It will stop eventually. Try not to worry," he advised.

Hannah hiccuped the whole way home.

On the fourth day of Hanukkah, Señora Rivera knocked on the Hartmans' door. "Hannah, *querida*. In Mexico we chase away *un ataque de hipos* with this," she said.

"Stick it between your eyes."

Hannah placed a wet, red string on her forehead.

"I feel silly," Hannah said. Henry giggled. Together they counted to ten in Spanish.

"**HICCUP!** Thanks—**HIC**—anyway," Hannah said, as Señora Rivera pulled the door closed behind her.

"Mom, I can't—**HIC**—sing with these hiccups!"

"I'm sure they'll go away," Mom said, squeezing her hand. But Hannah wasn't sure. She practiced her solo.

"I WON'T sing unless my hiccups go—**HIC**—away!" Hannah announced, stomping to her bedroom.

She hiccuped through the night, even in her dreams.

Hic!
Hic!
Hic!

On the fifth day of Hanukkah, Amar from the second floor brought cardamom cookies and ginger ale.

Hannah nibbled on a cookie and passed one to Henry. "**HICCUP!**" Everyone sighed.

On the sixth night of Hanukkah, the kids grated potatoes and onions for latkes.

While Mom fried the latkes, Hannah and Henry spooned applesauce and sour cream into bowls. Hannah's hiccups echoed like noisy crickets.

In the apartment below, Mrs. Morella thumped on her ceiling.

"Try peanut butter!" she shouted into her chandelier.

I'll try anything, Hannah thought. She slathered her latkes with peanut butter.

"Yuck," Henry said.

Hannah grimaced as she placed a forkful of peanut butter latke into her mouth.

She hiccuped louder. "What—**HIC**—am I going to do?" Hannah asked, sighing. Babka hid behind the drapes. Mom sat with her head in her hands. Henry finished everyone's latkes.

On the seventh night of her hiccuping Hanukkah, Hannah was so worried about her solo that she couldn't enjoy opening her gifts. Even Henry's silly faces didn't make her smile.
She snuggled Babka as she hiccuped through the night.

The next morning, their neighbor Mrs. Doukas brought Hannah pomegranate juice with mint. Though she didn't expect it to work, Hannah sipped anyway. "**HICCUP!**" She hugged Mrs. Doukas as she left.

Hannah sank into the couch with Babka, frowning. "Everyone will—**HIC**—laugh at me if I—**HIC**—sing with hiccups. I've tried *every*—**HIC**—thing!"

"Maybe no one will notice," Henry said. Hannah rolled her eyes.

"Your school is counting on you, Hannah. You have to try," Dad urged.

"Fine!" Hannah trudged into her room to dress for the show, with Babka at her heels.

She pulled her favorite sparkly dress over her head, still hiccuping. Babka crawled under her desk, barking. Hannah hiccuped as she brushed her hair. Babka howled.

"Are you—**HIC**—stuck again, Babka?" She bent to help him. And then Hannah had an idea. She decided she'd perform, hiccups or no hiccups.

Later, Hannah wrung her hands as she waited backstage. The music began, and she tiptoed to center stage. "**HICCUP!**" The audience giggled. Hannah grinned. She took a deep breath, started singing, and tapped across the stage.

No one heard Hannah's hiccups over the sound of her tapping toes and heels. She spun like a dreidel, finishing her dance with a great tapping shuffle across the stage.

Everyone clapped and cheered, and Hannah grinned as she took a hiccuping bow.

That night at home, Hannah's family invited their neighbors to join their Hanukkah celebration.

The neighbors gathered close as Hannah lit the menorah and Henry recited the blessings. As the candles glowed and flickered, Hannah hiccuped one last, loud, long Hanukkah **HICCUP**.

And then . . . her hiccups stopped. “Finally!” Hannah said, clapping her hands. “I hope that never happens again.”

“Me, too,” Henry said, giggling. “Next time you’ll probably get the Sukkot sneezes.”

A Note for Families

Hannah's Hanukkah hiccups lasted eight whole nights—just like the holiday of Hanukkah!

On Hanukkah, we join together to light our menorahs, spin our dreidels, and celebrate miracles that occurred long ago.

No one knows why Hannah's hiccups started, why they wouldn't go away, or why they finally stopped. All Hannah knows is that she has to figure out a way to perform her Hanukkah solo—even while hiccuping. And she does!

- What would you have done in Hannah's situation?
- Can you think of a time when you planned to do something special but then had to change your plans? How did that feel?
- Hannah's neighbors share their traditions to try to help cure her hiccups. In what ways do the people you know help one another?
- What can you do to help others this Hanukkah?

Wishing you a hiccup-free holiday.